OLD RHYMES
FOR ALL TIMES

Collected and Illustrated by
Cicely Mary Barker

Frederick Warne

Acknowledgements

The publishers would like to thank the following copyright holders for their permission to reproduce the copyright material in this book:

The Society of Authors as the literary representative of the Estate of Rose Fyleman for 'A Fairy Went A-Marketing'; Peters Fraser & Dunlop Group Ltd for 'The Yak' by Hilaire Belloc; David Higham Associates and Harold Ober Associates Inc. for 'Mary and Her Kitten' and 'Bubbles' by Eleanor Farjeon from *Tunes of a Penny Piper* published by William Collins Sons & Co. Ltd; The Literary Trustees of Walter de la Mare and the Society of Authors as their representative for 'Berries', 'Listen' and 'The Three Beggars'; The Bodley Head Ltd for 'Four-Paws' by Helen Parry Eden.

Every attempt has been made to trace the copyright holders of the poems in this book. The publishers apologise if any inadvertent omissions have been made.

FREDERICK WARNE

Published by the Penguin Group
Penguin Books Ltd, 27 Wrights Lane, London W8 5TZ, England
Penguin Books USA Inc., 375 Hudson Street, New York, N.Y. 10014, USA
Penguin Books Australia Ltd, Ringwood, Victoria, Australia
Penguin Books Canada Ltd, 10 Alcorn Avenue, Toronto, Ontario, Canada M4V 3B2
Penguin Books (N.Z.) Ltd, 182-190 Wairau Road, Auckland 10, New Zealand

Penguin Books Ltd, Registered Offices: Harmondsworth, Middlesex, England

First published 1928
This new revised edition first published 1993
1 3 5 7 9 10 8 6 4 2

Text and original illustrations copyright © The Estate of Cicely Mary Barker, 1928, 1933
New reproductions copyright © The Estate of Cicely Mary Barker, 1993
Copyright in all countries signatory to the Berne and Universal Conventions

ISBN 0 7232 4123 6

Colour reproduction by Saxon Photolitho Ltd, Norwich

Printed and bound in Great Britain by
William Clowes Limited, Beccles and London

CONTENTS

To
My Mother
Who read me so many Rhymes

BARLEY BRIDGE
A SINGING GAME.

Q. How many miles to Barley Bridge?
A. *Fourscore miles and ten!*
Q. Shall we be there by candle-light?
A. *Yes, and back again;*
If your heels are nimble and light,
You may get there by candle-light.
Q. Open the gates as wide as wide,
And let King George go through with his bride!
A courtsey to you, and a courtsey to you,
If you please, will you let the king's horses go
through?

Rosy apple, lemon or pear,
Bunch of roses she shall wear;
Gold and silver by her side,
I know who will be the bride.
Take her by the lily-white hand,
Lead her to the altar,
Give her kisses, one, two, three,
Mother's runaway daughter.

RING-A-RING O' ROSES

Ring-a-ring o' roses,
A pocket full of posies,
A-tishoo! A-tishoo!
We all fall down.

And you shall have a knife and fork
To eat with, like your betters

TINGLE-TANGLE TITMOUSE

Come hither, little piggy-wig,
Come and learn your letters,
And you shall have a knife and fork
To eat with, like your betters.
"Oh no," the little pig replied,
"My trough will do as well;
I'd rather eat my victuals there
Than learn to read and spell."

With a tingle-tangle titmouse,
  Robin knows great A,
B and C and D and E,
  F,G, H, I, J, K.

Come hither, little pussy cat;
If you will grammar study,
I'll give you silver clogs to wear
Whene'er the weather's muddy.
"Oh, if I grammar learn," said Puss,
"Your house will in a trice
Be overrun from top to bottom
With the rats and mice."

With a tingle-tangle titmouse,
  Robin knows great A,
B and C and D and E,
  F, G, H, I, J, K.

Come hither, little puppy-dog;
I'll give you a new collar
If you will learn to read and spell
And be a clever scholar.
"Oh no," the little dog replied,
"I've other fish to fry,
For I must learn to guard the house
And bark when thieves are nigh."

With a tingle-tangle titmouse,
  Robin knows great A,
B and C and D and E,
  F, G, H, I, J, K.

Then to my ten shillings
Add you but a groat

ABOUT THE BUSH

About the bush, Willie,
    About the bee-hive,
About the bush, Willie,
    I'll meet thee alive.

Then to my ten shillings
    Add you but a groat,
I'll go to Newcastle
    And buy a new coat.

Five and five shillings,
    Five and a crown;
Five and five shillings
    Will buy a new gown.

Five and five shillings,
    Five and a groat;
Five and five shillings
    Will buy a new coat.

A PAIL OF WATER.

A Singing Game

Draw a pail of water
For my lady's daughter,
My father's a king, and my mother's a queen,
My two little sisters are dressed in green,
Stamping grass and parsley,
Marigold leaves and daisies.
One rush, two rush,
Prythee, fine lady, come under my bush.

16

COUNTING

One, two, three, four,
Mary at the cottage door,
Eating cherries off a plate,
Five, six, seven, eight.

CHERRY STONES

Tinker, tailor,
Soldier, sailor,
Rich man, poor man,
Gentleman, farmer,
Apothecary,
Ploughboy,
Thief.

THE TWELVE OXEN
A very old rhyme

I have twelve oxen that be fair and brown,
And they go a-grazing down by the town;
With hey! with how! with hoy!
Sawest not you mine oxen, you little pretty boy?

I have twelve oxen, and they be fair and white,
And they go a-grazing down by the dyke,
With hey! with how! with hoy!
Sawest not you mine oxen, you little pretty boy?

I have twelve oxen, and they be fair and black,
And they go a-grazing down by the lake,
With hey! with how! with hoy!
Sawest not you mine oxen, you little pretty boy?

I have twelve oxen, and they be fair and red,
And they go a-grazing down by the mead.
With hey! with how! with hoy!
Sawest not you mine oxen, you little pretty boy?

Sawest not you mine oxen, you little pretty boy?

THE WIND

Who has seen the wind?
    Neither I nor you:
But when the leaves hang trembling
    The wind is passing thro'.

Who has seen the wind?
    Neither you nor I:
But when the trees bow down their heads
    The wind is passing by.

Christina G. Rossetti

An APPLE-TREE Rhyme
To be Sung in Orchards, at the New Year.

Here stands a good apple tree;
Stand fast at root,
Bear well at top;
Every little twig
Bear an apple big;
Every little bough
Bear an apple now;
Hats full! caps full!
Three-score sacks full!
Hullo, boys! hullo!

Airymouse, Airymouse, fly over my head

THE BAT

Airymouse, Airymouse, fly over my head,
And you shall have a crust o' bread;
And when I brew and when I bake,
You shall have a piece of my wedding-cake.

THE CUCKOO

The cuckoo's a bonny bird, he whistles as he flies,
He brings us good tidings, he tells us no lies;
He drinks the cold water to make his voice clear,
And when he sings cuckoo the summer is near;
Sings cuckoo in April, cuckoo in May,
Cuckoo in June, and then flies away.

ST. VALENTINE'S DAY

14th February

Good morrow to you, Valentine,
Please to give me a Valentine.
I'll be yourn, if ye'll be mine:
Good morrow to you, Valentine.

SHROVE TUESDAY — PANCAKE DAY.
A Begging Rhyme.

Knick a knock upon the block;
Flour and lard is very dear,
Please we come a-shroving here.
Your pan's hot and my pan's cold,
Hunger makes us shrovers bold:
Please to give poor shrovers something here.

MOTHERING SUNDAY

Simnel Sunday – Mid Lent

On Mothering Sunday, above all other,
Every child should dine with its mother.

*Note – A Simnel Cake is the proper present for
a daughter to bring her mother on this Sunday.*

THE MAYERS' SONG

We've been a-rambling all this night,
    And sometime of this day;
And now returning back again
    We bring a branch of May.

A branch of May we bring you here,
    And at your door it stands;
It is a sprout well budded out,
    The work of the Lord's hands.

The hedges and trees they are so green,
    As green as any leek;
Our Heavenly Father, He watered them
    With His heavenly dew so sweet.

The heavenly gates are open wide,
    Our paths are beaten plain;
And if a man be not too far gone,
    He may return again.

So dear, so dear as Christ loved us,
    And for our sins was slain,
Christ bids us turn from wickedness
    Back to the Lord again.

The moon shines bright, the stars give a light,
    A little before it is day,
So God bless you all, both great and small,
    And send you a joyful May.

And now returning back again
We bring a branch of May

HOT-CROSS BUNS

Hot-cross buns! Hot-cross buns!
One a penny, two a penny,
    Hot-cross buns!
If you have no daughters,
Give them to your sons,
One a penny, two a penny,
    Hot-cross buns!
But if you have none of these little elves,
Then you may eat them all yourselves.

MARCH DUST

The teacher said our hands weren't clean –
    I don't suppose they were –
But we'd been skipping on the green
    And nothing mattered there.

O, have you ever skipped in March
    Beneath the dappled skies,
And felt the grey dust dry and parch
    Your throat, and blind your eyes?

The schoolroom desks are old and worn;
    Our teacher doesn't know
That always on a bright March morn
    The fairy trumpets blow.

The hazel catkins and the larch
    Are waiting in the wood,
And celandines, the gold of March,
    Are bursting into bud.

On Saturday we'll roam beyond
    The farm upon the hill,
And feed the ducks upon the pond
    Beside the little mill;

But Monday soon will come again,
    And back to school we'll go;
But, peeping through the window pane,
    We'll see the March dust blow.

M. Derwin

Bring the comb and play upon it!
Marching, here we come!

MARCHING SONG

Bring the comb and play upon it!
  Marching, here we come!
Willie cocks his highland bonnet,
  Johnnie beats the drum.

Mary Jane commands the party,
  Peter leads the rear;
Feet in time, alert and hearty,
  Each a Grenadier!

All in the most martial manner
  Marching double-quick;
While the napkin like a banner
  Waves upon the stick!

Here's enough of fame and pillage,
  Great commander Jane!
Now that we've been round the village,
  Let's go home again.

Robert Louis Stevenson

HARVEST HOME

The boughs do shake and the bells do ring,
So merrily comes our harvest in,
Our harvest in, our harvest in,
So merrily comes our harvest in.

We have ploughed, and we have sowed,
We have reaped, and we have mowed,
We have brought home every load,
Hip, hip, hip,
    Harvest Home!

St. CLEMENT'S DAY — 23rd November.

Clemany! Clemany! Clemany mine!
A good red apple, a pint of wine,
Some of your mutton and some of your veal,
If it is good, pray give me a deal.
An apple, a pear, a plum or a cherry,
Any good thing to make us merry;
A bouncing buck and a velvet chair,
Clemany comes but once a year.
Off with the pot and on with the pan;
A good red apple and I'll be gone.

A NEW YEAR'S RHYME

Wassail, wassail, to our town,
The cup is white, the ale is brown;
The cup is made of the ashen tree,
And so is your ale of the good barley.
Little maid, little maid, turn the pin,
Open the door and let us come in.
God be here, God be there,
I wish you all a happy New Year.

Note –The Wassail Cup was a wooden cup (one rhyme says "made of the rosemary tree") of spiced ale, apples and sugar, which they drank at the New Year. The word Wassail comes from the Anglo-Saxon Wæs hâl! be whole! – that is to say, good health to you! Children carried round a bunch of evergreens hung with apples, oranges and ribbons, called a Wessel-bob. "Turn the pin" means "unfasten the latch".

THE WASSAIL SONG

Here we come a-wassailing
Among the leaves so green;
Here we come a-wandering,
So fair to be seen:

  Love and joy come to you,
  And to you your wassail too,
  And God bless you and send you
    A happy New Year.

34

Wassail, wassail, to our town

We are not daily beggars
That beg from door to door,
But we are neighbours' children,
Whom you have seen before.

The roads are very dirty,
Our shoes are very thin;
We've got a little pocket
To put a penny in.

God bless the master of this house,
Likewise the mistress too,
And all the little children,
That round the table go.

Good Master and Mistress,
While you're sitting by the fire,
Pray think of us poor children
Who are wandering in the mire.

Love and joy come to you,
And to you your wassail too,
And God bless you and send you
A happy New Year.

ST. SWITHIN'S DAY

15th July

St. Swithin's Day, if thou dost rain,
For forty days it will remain;
St. Swithin's Day, if thou be fair,
For forty days 't will rain na mair.

THE RAIN

Rain on the green grass,
 And rain on the tree,
And rain on the house-top,
 But not upon me!

Bread and milk for breakfast,
And woollen frocks to wear

A CAROL SINGER'S RHYME

Knock at the knocker,
　　ring at the bell,
Ask for a penny
　　for singing so well;
If you ain't got a penny, a ha'penny will do;
If you ain't got a ha'penny,
　　God bless *you!*

WINTER

Bread and milk for breakfast,
And woollen frocks to wear,
And a crumb for robin redbreast
On the cold days of the year.

Christina G. Rossetti

COCK ROBIN AND JENNY WREN.

Little Jenny Wren
Fell sick upon a time;
Robin came to see her,
And brought her cake and wine.

"Eat well your cake, Jenny,
Drink well your wine."
"Yes, kind Robin,
And you shall be mine."

Jenny she got well again
And stood upon her feet,
And she told poor Robin
She loved him not a bit.

Robin he was angry
And hopped upon a twig,
Saying, "Out upon you, fie upon you,
Bold-faced jig!"

THE CLEVER HEN

I had a little hen, the prettiest ever seen,
She washed me the dishes, and kept the house clean.
She went to the mill to fetch me some flour,
She brought it home in less than an hour.
She baked me my bread, she brewed me my ale,
She sat by the fire and told many a fine tale.

A FAIRY WENT A-MARKETING

A fairy went a-marketing –
   She bought a little fish;
She put it in a crystal bowl
   Upon a golden dish.
An hour she sat in wonderment
   And watched its silver gleam,
And then she gently took it up
   And slipped it in a stream.

A fairy went a-marketing –
   She bought a coloured bird;
It sang the sweetest, shrillest song
   That ever she had heard.
She sat beside its painted cage
   And listened half the day,
And then she opened wide the door
   And let it fly away.

A fairy went a-marketing –
   She bought a winter gown
All stitched about with gossamer
   And lined with thistledown.
She wore it all the afternoon
   With prancing and delight,
Then gave it to a little frog
   To keep him warm at night.

And then she kissed its silken ears

A fairy went a-marketing –
　　She bought a gentle mouse
To take her tiny messages,
　　To keep her tiny house.
All day she kept its busy feet
　　Pit-patting to and fro,
And then she kissed its silken ears,
　　Thanked it, and let it go.

Rose Fyleman

THE
BIRDS

A SUSSEX RHYME

Robins and wrens
Are God Almighty's friends;
Martins and swallows
Are God Almighty's scholars.

(I am afraid you must say "swallers" to make this rhyme!)

THE ROBINS

A robin and a robin's son
Once went to town to buy a bun.
They couldn't decide on plum or plain,
And so they went back home again.

LITTLE TROTTY WAGTAIL

Little trotty wagtail, he went in the rain,
And twittering, tottering sideways
he ne'er got straight again.
He stooped to get a worm, and looked up to get a fly,
And then he flew away ere his feathers they were dry.

Little trotty wagtail, he waddled in the mud;
And left his little footmarks, trample where he would.
He waddled in the water-pudge,
and waggle went his tail,
And chirrup up his wings to dry upon the garden rail.

Little trotty wagtail, you nimble all about,
And in the dimpling water-pudge
you waddle in and out;
Your home is nigh at hand and in the warm pig-stye,
So little Master Wagtail, I'll bid you a good-bye.

John Clare

Mab will pinch her by the toe

THE FAIRIES

If ye will with Mab find grace,
Set each Platter in his place:
Rake the Fire up, and get
Water in; ere Sun be set.
Wash your Pails, and cleanse your Dairies;
Sluts are loathsome to the Fairies:
Sweep your house: Who doth not so,
Mab will pinch her by the toe.

Robert Herrick

THE YAK

As a friend to the children, commend me the Yak.
    You will find it exactly the thing:
It will carry and fetch, you can ride on its back,
    Or lead it about with a string.

The Tartar who dwells on the plains of Tibet
    (A desolate region of snow),
Has for centuries made it a nursery pet,
    And surely the Tartar should know!

Then tell your papa where the Yak can be got,
    And if he is awfully rich
He will buy you the creature – or else he will *not*.
    (I cannot be positive which.)

Hilaire Belloc

MARY AND HER KITTEN

The Kitten's in the Dairy!
Where's our Mary?
She isn't in the Kitchen,
She isn't at her Stitching,
She isn't at the Weeding,
The Brewing, or the Kneading!
Mary's in the Garden, walking in a Dream
Mary's got her Fancies, and the Kitten's got the Cream.

Eleanor Farjeon

LAMBKINS

On the grassy banks
Lambkins at their pranks;
Woolly sisters, woolly brothers,
Jumping off their feet,
While their woolly mothers
Watch by them and bleat.

Christina G. Rossetti

BERRIES

There was an old woman
      Went blackberry picking
Along the hedges
      From Weep to Wicking.
Half a pottle –
      No more had she got,
When out steps a Fairy
      From her green grot;
And says, "Well, Jill,
      Would 'ee pick 'ee mo?"
And Jill, she curtseys,
      And looks just so.
"Be off," says the Fairy,
      "As quick as you can,
Over the meadows
      To the little green lane,
That dips to the hayfields
      Of Farmer Grimes:
I've berried those hedges
      A score of times;

When out steps a Fairy
From her green grot

Bushel on bushel
        I'll promise 'ee, Jill,
This side of supper
        If 'ee pick with a will."
She glints very bright,
        And speaks her fair;
Then lo, and behold!
        She had faded in air.

Be sure Old Goodie
        She trots betimes
Over the meadows
        To Farmer Grimes.
And never was queen
        With jewellery rich
As those same hedges
        From twig to ditch;
Like Dutchman's coffers,
        Fruit, thorn, and flower –
They shone like William
        And Mary's bower.
And be sure Old Goodie
        Went back to Weep,
So tired with her basket
        She scarce could creep.

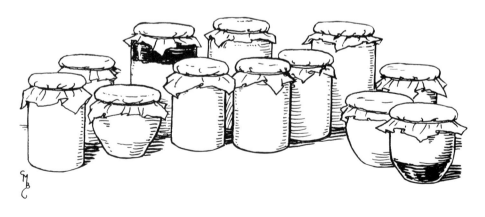

When she comes in the dusk
    To her cottage door,
There's Towser wagging
    As never before,
To see his Missus
    So glad to be
Come from her fruit-picking
    Back to he.

As soon as next morning
    Dawn was grey,
The pot on the hob
    Was simmering away;
And all in a stew
    And a hugger-mugger
Towser and Jill
    A-boiling of sugar,
And the dark clear fruit
    That from Faërie came,
For syrup and jelly
    And blackberry jam.

Twelve jolly gallipots
    Jill put by;
And one little teeny one,
    One inch high;
And that she's hidden
    A good thumb deep,
Halfway over
    From Wicking to Weep.

Walter de la Mare

Speak a little louder, sir, I'm very hard of hearin'

THE DEAF OLD WOMAN

"Old woman, old woman, wilt thee go a-shearing'?"
"Speak a little louder, sir, I'm very hard of hearin'."

"Old woman, old woman, wilt thee go a-gleanin'?"
"Speak a little louder, I canna tell the meanin'!"

"Old woman, old woman, wilt thee go a-walkin'?"
"Speak a little louder, or what's the use o' talkin'!"

"Old woman, old woman, shall I kiss thee dearly?"
"Thank you, kind sir, I hear you very clearly!"

BABY

My baby has a mottled fist,
My baby has a neck in creases;
My baby kisses and is kissed,
For he's the very thing for kisses.

Christina G. Rossetti

THE FAERIE FAIR

The fairies hold a fair, they say,
Beyond the hills when skies are grey
And daylight things are laid away.

And very strange their marketing,
If we could see them on the wing
With all the fairy ware they bring.

Long strings they sell, of berries bright,
And wet wind-fallen apples light
Blown from the trees some starry night.

Gay patches, too, for tattered wings,
Gold bubbles blown by goblin things,
And mushrooms for the fairy rings.

Fine flutes are there, of magic reed,
Whose piping sets the elves indeed
A-dancing down the dewy mead.

These barter they for bats and moles,
For beaten silver bells and bowls,
Bright from the caverns of the Trolls.

And so they show, and sell and buy,
With song and dance right merrily,
Until the morning gilds the sky.

Florence Harrison

THE CHESTNUT COLT

My chestnut colt with the fairies grew,
They shod each hoof with a silver shoe;
He jumps and trots as my fair maid rides,
For twenty long miles – and more besides!

Jennett Humphreys (Translated from Old Welsh)

SOLDIER, SOLDIER

"O soldier, soldier, won't you marry me,
  With your musket, fife, and drum?"
"Ah, no! sweet maid, I cannot marry thee,
  For I have no coat to put on."
Then up she went to her grandfather's chest,
And brought him a coat of the very, very best:
She brought him a coat of the very, very best,
    And the soldier put it on.

"O soldier, soldier, won't you marry me,
  With your musket, fife, and drum?"
"Ah, no! sweet maid, I cannot marry thee,
  For I have no boots to put on."
Then up she went to her grandfather's chest,
And brought him a pair of the very, very best:
She brought him a pair of the very, very best,
    And the soldier put them on.

Ah, no! sweet maid, I cannot marry thee,
For I have no coat to put on

"O soldier, soldier, won't you marry me,
  With your musket, fife, and drum?"
"Ah, no! sweet maid, I cannot marry thee,
  For I have no hat to put on."
Then up she went to her grandfather's chest,
And brought him a hat of the very, very best:
She brought him a hat of the very, very best,
    And the soldier put it on.

"Now, soldier, soldier, won't you marry me,
  With your musket, fife, and drum?"
"Ah, no! sweet maid, I cannot marry thee,
  For I have a wife of my own!"
And that's why the soldier cannot marry thee,
    With his musket, fife, and drum.
Yes, that's why the soldier cannot marry thee,
    For he has a wife of his own!

 A WARNING

The robin and the redbreast,
The robin and the wren,
If ye take from their nest,
Ye'll never thrive again.

The robin and the redbreast,
The martin and the swallow,
If ye touch one of their eggs,
Bad luck will surely follow.

WEATHER WISDOM

To foretell a hard winter

Many haws, many sloes:
Many cold toes.

To know the sky

Red in the morning,
Shepherd's warning;
Red at night,
Shepherd's delight.

Blowing Bubbles! See how fine!

BUBBLES

Blowing Bubbles! See how fine!
Look at Mine! O look at Mine!
How they dance, and how they shine –
Mine! Mine! Look at Mine!
Mine's like Water! Mine's like Wine!
Yours is not as big as Mine!

Eleanor Farjeon

THE MAN THEY MADE

We made a Man all by ourselves;
   We made him jolly fat;
We stuck a Pipe into his face,
   And on his head a Hat.

We made him stand upon one Leg,
   That so he might not walk,
We made his Mouth without a Tongue,
   That so he might not talk.

We left him grinning on the Lawn
   That we to Bed might go;
But in the night he ran away, –
   Leaving a heap of snow!

Hamish Hendry

PATCHES

Better a clout
Than a hole out.

HOW TO SOW BEANS

One for the mouse, one for the crow,
One to rot, and one to grow.

PLOUGHING

Plough deep while sluggards sleep,
And you shall have corn to sell and keep.

LAVENDER'S BLUE.

Lavender's blue, diddle diddle, lavender's green,
When I am king, diddle diddle, you shall be queen.

Who told you so, diddle diddle, who told you so?
'Twas my own heart, diddle diddle, that told me so.

Call up your men, diddle diddle, set them to work,
Some with a rake, didle diddle, some with a fork,

Some to make hay, diddle diddle, some to thresh corn,
Whilst you and I, diddle diddle, keep ourselves warm.

LISTEN!

Quiet your faces; be crossed every thumb;
  Fix on me deep your eyes!
And out of my mind a story shall come,
  Old, lovely, and wise.

Old as the pebbles that fringe the cold seas;
  Lovely as apples in rain;
Wise as that King who learned of the bees,
  Then learned of the emmets again.

Old as the fruits that in mistletoe shine,
  Lovely as amber, as snow;
Wise as the fool who, when care made him pine,
  Sang, Heh, fol lol, lilly lo!

Old as the woods rhyming Thomas snuffed sweet,
  When pillion he rid with the Queen;
Lovely as elf-craft; wise as the street
  Where the roofs of the humble are seen...

Hsst! there's a stirring, there's a wind in the snow;
  A whirring of birds on the wing,
Like a river of water my story shall flow,
  Like runnels of water sing.

Walter de la Mare

Fix on me deep your eyes!

Come, butter, come;
Come, butter, come;
Peter stands at the gate
Waiting for a buttered cake;
Come, butter, come!

THE FIRST OF MAY

The fair maid who, the first of May,
Goes to the fields at break of day,
And washes in dew from the hawthorn tree,
Will ever after handsome be.

John and his Mare.

John and his mare a journey went,
     Humble, dumble, derry derry dee;
They travelled slow, by joint consent,
     Tweedle, tweedle, tweedle, twinery.

They travelled near a hundred miles,
     Humble, dumble, derry derry dee;
The mare jumped over all the stiles,
     Tweedle, tweedle, tweedle, twinery.

It rained and blew as night came on,
     Humble, dumble, derry derry dee;
Said John, "I wish we were at home,"
     Tweedle, tweedle, tweedle, twinery.

Then said the mare, "What shall we do?
    Humble, dumble, derry derry dee,
"Good Master, I have lost a shoe."
    Tweedle, tweedle, tweedle, twinery.

"Alack!" said John, "where can we stop?
    Humble, dumble, derry derry dee,
I do not see a blacksmith's shop."
    Tweedle, tweedle, tweedle, twinery.

At length they came to a great hall,
    Humble, dumble, derry derry dee,
Where John did loudly knock and call.
    Tweedle, tweedle, tweedle, twinery.

The King came out all dressed so gay,
    Humble, dumble, derry derry dee,
And begged to know what he'd to say.
    Tweedle, tweedle, tweedle, twinery.

Says John, "I'm wet, Sir, to the skin."
        Humble dumble, derry derry dee.
Then said the King, "Pray, sir, step in."
        Tweedle, tweedle, tweedle, twinery.

The King brought a dry shirt for John,
        Humble, dumble, derry derry dee,
And helped him to put it on.
        Tweedle, tweedle, tweedle, twinery.

He introduced him to the Queen.
Humble, dumble, derry derry dee,
As fair a dame as e'er was seen.
Tweedle, tweedle, tweedle, twinery.

He gave him supper and a bed,
Humble dumble, derry derry dee,
And ordered that his horse be fed.
Tweedle, tweedle, tweedle, twinery.

So well did John behave him there,
Humble, dumble, derry derry dee,
The King and Queen made him Lord Mayor.
Tweedle, tweedle, tweedle, twinery.

And now John's got a coach and four,
Humble, dumble, derry derry dee,
I'll end my song, and sing no more
Tweedle, tweedle, tweedle, twinery.

THE PRINCESS AND HER SHOE

Doodle, doodle, doo,
The princess lost her shoe;
The princess hopped.
The fiddler stopped,
Not knowing what to do.

DAME TROT AND HER CAT

Dame Trot and her cat,
Sat down for to chat,
The Dame sat on this side,
And Puss sat on that.

"Puss," says the Dame,
"Can you catch a rat,
Or a mouse in the dark?"
"Purr," says the cat.

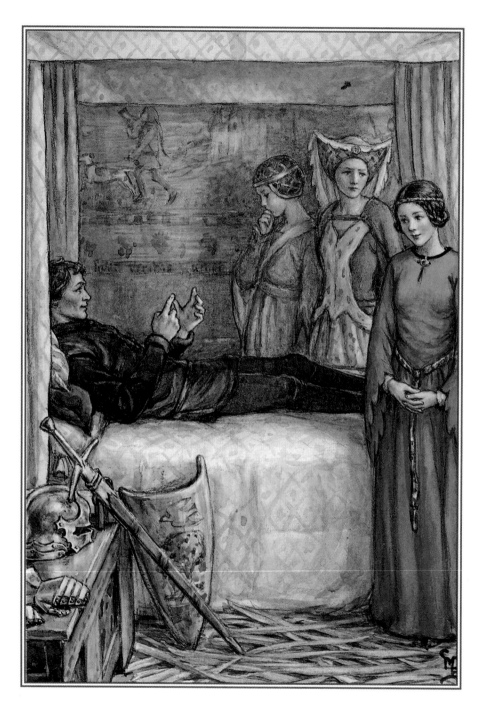

And if you can answer questions three,
O then, fair maid, I'll marry wi' thee

THE RIDDLING KNIGHT

I
There were three sisters fair and bright,
   Jennifer, Gentle, and Rosemary,
And they three loved one valiant knight
   As the dow[1] flies over the mulberry tree.

II
The eldest sister let him in,
And barr'd the door with a silver pin.

III
The second sister made his bed,
And placed soft pillows under his head.

IV
The youngest sister that same night
Was resolved to wed wi' this valiant knight.

V
The Knight: "And if you can answer questions three,
   O then, fair maid, I'll marry wi' thee.

VI
"O what is louder than a horn,
Or what is sharper than a thorn?

VII
"Or what is heavier than the lead,
Or what is better than the bread?

[1]*Dow,* dove

75

VII

"Or what is longer than the way,
Or what is deeper than the sea?"

IX

Rosemary: "O shame is louder than a horn,
And hunger is sharper than a thorn.

X

"O sin is heavier than the lead,
The blessing's better than the bread.

XI

"O the wind is longer than the way,
And love is deeper than the sea."

XII

The Knight: "You have answer'd aright my questions three,
Jennifer, Gentle, and Rosemary;
And now, fair maid, I'll marry wi' thee,"
As the dow flies over the mulberry tree.

Note - Such a very old rhyme as this, which was sung and said for hundreds of years before ever it was written down, changing bit by bit as this person forgot something and the next person made up something a little different, is rather like a worn penny, so much rubbed away that you can hardly tell what it said or looked like when it was new. But you may be pretty sure we are meant to think that the Knight was ready to marry whichever of the sisters could guess his riddles, and that Rosemary was the one who did guess them.

GOOD MANNERS FOR MEAL TIMES

Of a little take a little,
  Manners so to do;
Of a little leave a little;
  That is manners, too.

TOO QUIET

When children stand still
They have done some ill.

THE THREE BEGGARS

'Twas autumn daybreak gold and wild,
  While past St. Ann's grey tower they shuffled,
Three beggars spied a fairy-child
  In crimson mantle muffled.

The daybreak lighted up her face
  All pink, and sharp, and emerald-eyed;
She looked on them a little space,
  And shrill as hautboy cried: –

"O three tall footsore men of rags
  Which walking this gold morn I see,
What will ye give me from your bags
  For fairy kisses three?"

The first, that was a reddish man,
  Out of his bundle takes a crust:
"La, by the tombstones of St. Ann
  There's fee, if fee ye must!"

The second, that was a chestnut man,
  Out of his bundle draws a bone:
"La, by the belfry of St. Ann,
  And all my breakfast gone!"

The third, that was a yellow man,
  Out of his bundle picks a groat,
"La, by the Angel of St. Ann,
  And I must go without."

What will ye give me from your bags?

That changeling, lean and icy-lipped,
  Touched crust, and bone, and groat, and lo!
Beneath her finger taper-tipped
  The magic all ran through.

Instead of crust a peacock pie,
  Instead of bone sweet venison,
Instead of groat a white lilie
  With seven blooms thereon.

And each fair cup was deep with wine:
  Such was the changeling's charity,
The sweet feast was enough for nine,
  But not too much for three.

O toothsome meat in jelly froze!
  O tender haunch of elfin stag!
O rich the odour that arose!
  O plump with scraps each bag!

There, in the daybreak gold and wild,
  Each merry-hearted beggar man
Drank deep unto the fairy child,
  And blessed the good St. Ann.

Walter de la Mare

80

OUT IN THE DARK

From "The Night-piece, to Julia"

Her eyes the glow-worm lend thee,
The shooting stars attend thee;
    And the Elves also,
    Whose little eyes glow
Like the sparks of fire, befriend thee.

No Will-o'-the-Wisp mis-light thee;
Nor snake or slow-worm bite thee:
    But on, on thy way
    Not making a stay,
Since ghost there's none to affright thee.

Let not the dark thee cumber;
What though the moon does slumber?
    The stars of the night
    Will lend thee their light,
Like tapers clear without number.

Robert Herrick

That's the way for Billy and me

THE WAY FOR BILLY AND ME

Where the pools are bright and deep,
Where the grey trout lies asleep,
Up the river and over the lea,
That's the way for Billy and me.

Where the blackbird sings the latest,
Where the hawthorn blooms the sweetest,
Where the nestlings chirp and flee,
That's the way for Billy and me.

Where the mowers mow the cleanest,
Where the hay lies thick and greenest;
There to track the homeward bee,
That's the way for Billy and me.

Where the hazel bank is steepest,
Where the shadow falls the deepest,
Where the clustering nuts fall free,
That's the way for Billy and me.

Why the boys should drive away
Little sweet maidens from the play,
Or love to banter and fight so well,
That's the thing I never could tell.

But this I know, I love to play
Through the meadow, among the hay;
Up the water and over the lea,
That's the way for Billy and me.

James Hogg

FOR BABY'S TOES

I

The pettitoes are little feet,
And the little feet not big;
Great feet belong to the grunting hog,
And the pettitoes to the little pig.

II

This little pig went to market,
This little pig stayed at home,
This little pig had roast beef,
This little pig had none.
And this little pig cried, wee – wee – wee
All the way home.

THE ECHOING GREEN

The sun does arise
And make happy the skies;
The merry bells ring
To welcome the Spring;
The skylark and thrush,
The birds of the bush,
Sing louder around
To the bells' cheerful sound;
While our sports shall be seen
On the echoing green.

Old John, with white hair,
Does laugh away care,
Sitting under the oak,
Among the old folk.
They laugh at our play,
And soon they all say,
"Such, such were the joys
When we were all – girls and boys –
In our youth-time were seen
On the echoing green."

Till the little ones, weary,
No more can be merry:
The sun does descend,
And our sports have an end.
Round the laps of their mothers
Many sisters and brothers,
Like birds in their nest,
Are ready for rest,
And sport no more seen
On the darkening green.

THIS IS THE WAY THE LADIES RIDE

This is the way the ladies ride,
Nim, nim, nim, nim.
This is the way the gentlemen ride,
Trim, trim, trim, trim.
This is the way the farmers ride,
Trot, trot, trot, trot.
This is the way the huntsmen ride,
A-gallop, a-gallop, a-gallop, a-gallop.
This is the way the ploughboys ride,
Hobble-dy-gee, hobble-dy-gee.

THREE PLUM BUNS

Three plum buns
    To eat here at the stile,
In the clover meadow,
    For we have walked a mile.

One for you, and one for me,
    And one left over:
Give it to the boy who shouts
    To scare the sheep from the clover.

Christina G. Rossetti

WHOLE DUTY OF CHILDREN

A child should always say what's true,
And speak when he is spoken to,
And behave mannerly at table:
At least as far as he is able.

Robert Louis Stevenson

THE NAUGHTY BOY

There was a naughty boy,
And a naughty boy was he,
He ran away to Scotland
The people for to see –
Then he found
That the ground
Was as hard,
That a yard
Was as long,
That a song
Was as merry,
That a cherry
Was as red –
That lead
Was as weighty,
That fourscore
Was as eighty,
That a door
Was as wooden
As in England –
So he stood in his shoes
And he wonder'd,
He wonder'd,
He stood in his shoes
And he wonder'd.

John Keats

THE LADY AND THE SWINE

There was a lady loved a swine,
   "Honey," quoth she,
"Pig-hog, wilt thou be mine?"
   "Humph!" quoth he.

"I'll build thee a silver sty,
   Honey," quoth she,
"And in it thou shalt lie."
   "Humph!" quoth he.

"Pinned with a silver pin,
   Honey," quoth she,
"That thou may'st go out and in."
   "Humph!" quoth he.

"Wilt thou now have me,
   Honey?" quoth she.
"Humph! humph! humph!" quoth he,
   And went his way.

But I by your cradle,
Dear baby, will keep

TWO HUSHABYES

I

Hush-a-bye, baby,
Nurse is away,
Sisters and brothers are gone out to play;
But I by your cradle,
Dear baby, will keep,
To guard you from danger and sing you to sleep.

II

Hush-a-bye, baby,
Pussy's a lady,
Mousie has gone to the mill;
And if you don't cry
She'll come back by and by,
So hush-a-bye, baby, lie still.

"FOUR-PAWS"

Four-Paws, the kitten from the farm,
 Is come to live with Betsey-Jane,
Leaving the stack-yard for the warm
 Flower-compassed cottage in the lane,
To wash his idle face and play
Among chintz cushions all the day.

Under the shadow of her hair
 He lies, who loves him nor desists
To praise his whiskers and compare
 The tabby bracelets on his wrists, –
Omelet at lunch and milk at tea
Suit Betsey-Jane and so fares he.

Happy beneath her golden hand
 He purrs contentedly nor hears
His Mother mourning through the land,

The old grey cat with tattered ears
And humble tail and heavy paw
Who brought him up among the straw.

Never by day she ventures nigh,
    But when the dusk grows dim and deep
And moths flit out of the strange sky
    And Betsey has been long asleep –
Out of the dark she comes and brings
Her dark maternal offerings; –

Some field-mouse or a throstle caught
    Near netted fruit or in the corn,
Or rat, for this her darling sought
    In the old barn where he was born;
And all lest on his dainty bed
Four-Paws were faint or under-fed.

Only between the twilight hours
    Under the window-panes she walks
Shrewdly among the scented flowers
    Nor snaps the soft nasturtium stalks,
Uttering still her plaintive cries
And Four-Paws, from the house, replies,

Leaps from his cushion to the floor,
    Down the brick passage scantly lit,
Waits wailing at the outer door
    Till one arise and open it –
Then from the swinging lantern's light
Runs to his Mother in the night.

Helen Parry Eden

Twinkle, twinkle little star,
How I wonder what you are!

TWINKLE, TWINKLE LITTLE STAR

Twinkle, twinkle little star,
How I wonder what you are!
Up above the world so high
Like a diamond in the sky.

When the blazing sun is gone,
When he nothing shines upon,
Then you show your little light,
Twinkle, twinkle, all the night.

In the dark blue sky you keep,
And often through my curtains peep,
For you never shut your eye
Till the sun is in the sky.

As your bright and tiny spark,
Lights the traveller in the dark,
Though I know not what you are,
Twinkle, twinkle, little star.

GOOD NIGHT

Pleasant dreams,
Sweet repose,
All the bed,
And all the clothes.

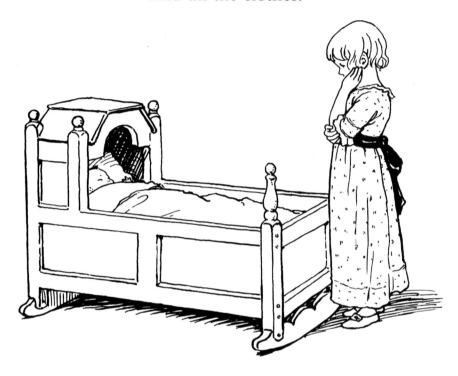